THE MUPPETS

Little, Brown and Company

Hachette Book Group
237 Park Avenue, New York, NY 10017
Visit our website at www.lb-kids.com

Little, Brown and Company is a division of Hachette Book Group, Inc.
The Little, Brown name and logo are trademarks of Hachette Book Group, Inc.

The publisher is not responsible for websites (or their content) that are not owned by the publisher.

First Edition: February 2013

ISBN 978-0-316-20133-9

10 9 8 7 6 5 4 3 2 1

Book design by Maria Mercado

IM

Printed in China

Disney

THE MUPPETS
Easter Eggstravaganza!

by Martha T. Ottersley
illustrated by Amy Mebberson

L B

LITTLE, BROWN AND COMPANY
New York   Boston

Do you ever have the funny, fuzzy, foggy feeling that you are forgetting something? Something super-extra-big-time-important?

Well, that's *exactly* the way Kermit the Frog feels this morning when he arrives at the Muppet Theater. Funny, fuzzy, foggy, and *froggy*. He puts his hand to his head, trying to remember—and then he sees a giant Easter egg on his desk!

Just then, Fozzie bursts in. "KERMIT! KERMIT! Look what the Easter Bunny left for me!"

"You got something, too?" asks Kermit.

"Yes!" says Fozzie. "Read this note. I feel like I'm forgetting something— Heeeey, nice bunny suit."

There's a note attached to the egg. It reads:

Dear Kermit,
Follow your nose and follow your eyes.
Inside this egg is a big surprise!

"Well, frogs don't really have noses," says Kermit. "But I hope it's chocolate dragonflies!" He opens the egg....

But it isn't chocolate dragonflies. It's a very silly bunny disguise!

"I guess the Easter Bunny forgot something, too," says Kermit. "Like how much I love chocolate dragonflies."

"Oh, Kermie! Kermie!" Miss Piggy shouts from her dressing room. Kermit and Fozzie look up to see what all the hubbub is about. Piggy has gotten a special Easter-egg surprise, too!

Kermit takes Fozzie's note and reads:

Dear Fozzie,
Open this egg, and you'll get a treat.
Easter without them is incomplete.
Too many of them could make you sick.
Can you guess what's inside?

"I think it's marshmallow chicks!"
says Fozzie.

But inside Fozzie's egg is a book of comedy tricks!
"*Jokes Before Yolks*!" says Fozzie, reading the title.
"Wow! This book has all sorts of great jokes."
Kermit doesn't even hear him. He is still trying to remember what he is forgetting.

"Look what the Easter Bunny left for *moi*!" she says, and reads the note to them.

Dear Miss Piggy,
Here is your Easter egg, filled just for *vous*,
With something that's French and a little foo-foo.
Guaranteed to reverse any frown...

"It must be a brand-new Easter gown!" sings Miss Piggy.

But it isn't. Instead it's a list of everyone in town!

"Note to self," says Miss Piggy. "Remember to SOCK the Easter Bunny next time I see him! Did he forget Easter is all about *moi* looking *fantastique*?"

"I don't know about the Easter Bunny," says Kermit, "but I'm one forgetful frog."

A moment later, Gonzo and Camilla stop by with yet ANOTHER giant Easter egg. "Look what we got!" shouts Gonzo as he starts to read the note attached to their egg.

Dear Gonzo and Camilla,
Red and yellow and pink and green,
Purple and orange and aquamarine.
It's every color that meets the eye
Because inside your egg is...

"A really tacky tie!" guesses Gonzo.
But it's not.

Inside their egg are two
dozen hard-boiled eggs and
Easter-egg dye!

"Baw...kaw?" asks Camilla.

"Yes, Camilla, I feel like
we're forgetting something, too,"
says Gonzo.

"What is wrong with the Easter Bunny this year?" shouts Miss Piggy. "It's like he forgot about all the things we like!"

"These aren't from the Easter Bunny!" says Scooter, appearing in the hallway with a giant egg-shaped package. "They're everything we need for tonight's special show, the Muppet Easter Eggstravaganza! Remember? We decided just yesterday to add this performance. Everything we need was delivered this morning—I just had some fun writing little poems about them. Happy Easter!"

Kermit looks at Fozzie.

Fozzie looks at Piggy.

Piggy looks at Gonzo.

Gonzo looks at Camilla.

Camilla looks at you, the reader.

"AAAAAAAAAAAAAAAAAAAH!!! *Now* we remember!" they cry.

The whole afternoon is a busy blur of Muppet mayhem! Gonzo and Camilla dye dozens of Easter eggs for Gonzo's big Dare-Deviled Egg stunt.

Miss Piggy personally autographs and kissy-kisses photos of herself for everyone in town.

Fozzie brushes up on all his Easter jokes. "Why did the Easter egg go to bed so early? He was EGGS-austed! Wocka! Wocka!"

And Kermit practices his brand-new banjo act, in full silly pink bunny costume.

The Muppet Easter Eggstravaganza is a huge hit! There are even surprise Easter baskets for everyone, with real Easter treats inside!

Kermit loves his chocolate dragonflies.

Fozzie shares his marshmallow chicks. (If he ate them all, he would feel a little sick!)

Miss Piggy is stunning in her new French Easter gown as she belts out a song.

And Gonzo performs his stunt in a really tacky tie!

You're Invited to the
MUPPET
EASTER
EGGSTRAVAGANZA!!

who: EVERYONE IN TOWN!
time: EASTER EVENING
place: the MUPPET THEATER
dress: (Yes, please get dressed.)

Happy Easter, everyone!

BAW-KAW!!!